Portville Free Library
Portville, New York 14770

BOXING
is for me

BOXING
is for me

Art Thomas
and Laura Storms

photographs by
Robert L. Wolfe

 Lerner Publications Company Minneapolis

The authors wish to thank the following for their help with this book: Roger Young; Dennis Ganley and the members of the Minneapolis Police Federation–Jerry Gamble's Boy's Club Boxing Team; Jim Kelly, P.A.L. #10, Cleveland, Ohio; and Mark Lerner.

Photographs on the following pages by Arnie Odessky: 39, 40 (right, top and bottom), 41-47

Editorial Consultant: Roger Young
                       Assistant Executive Director
                       and Region One Director
                       Upper Midwest Golden Gloves, Inc.

LIBRARY OF CONGRESS CATALOGING IN PUBLICATION DATA

Thomas, Art, 1952-
   Boxing is for me.

  (Sports for me books)
   Summary: Darren learns the techniques of boxing, including sparring, punching, and footwork, as well as the sport's safety rules.
   1. Boxing—Juvenile literature. [1. Boxing]
I. Storms, Laura. II. Wolfe, Robert L., ill.
III. Title. IV. Series.
GV1136.T46   796.8'3   81-15559
ISBN 0-8225-1133-9   AACR2

Copyright © 1982 by Lerner Publications Company

All rights reserved. International copyright secured. No part of this book may be reproduced in any form whatsoever without permission in writing from the publisher except for the inclusion of brief quotations in an acknowledged review.

Manufactured in the United States of America

International Standard Book Number: 0-8225-1133-9
Library of Congress Catalog Card Number: 81-15559

Hi! My name is Darren. The sport I enjoy most is boxing. In boxing, you try to land punches with your hands. You wear special gloves and box with an opponent.

5

You might think that boxing sounds dangerous. But the rules of the sport and special equipment, like the headgear and mouthpiece I'm wearing, make boxing very safe. It is a sport that takes a lot of skill and practice. I'd like to tell you about boxing and about how I became involved in this sport.

There's a gym near my house where boxers train. They are all **amateur** boxers. Amateurs do not get paid for boxing. They do it because they enjoy the sport. At the gym, the boxers work hard to get in shape. They do exercises, and they practice for **bouts,** or boxing matches.

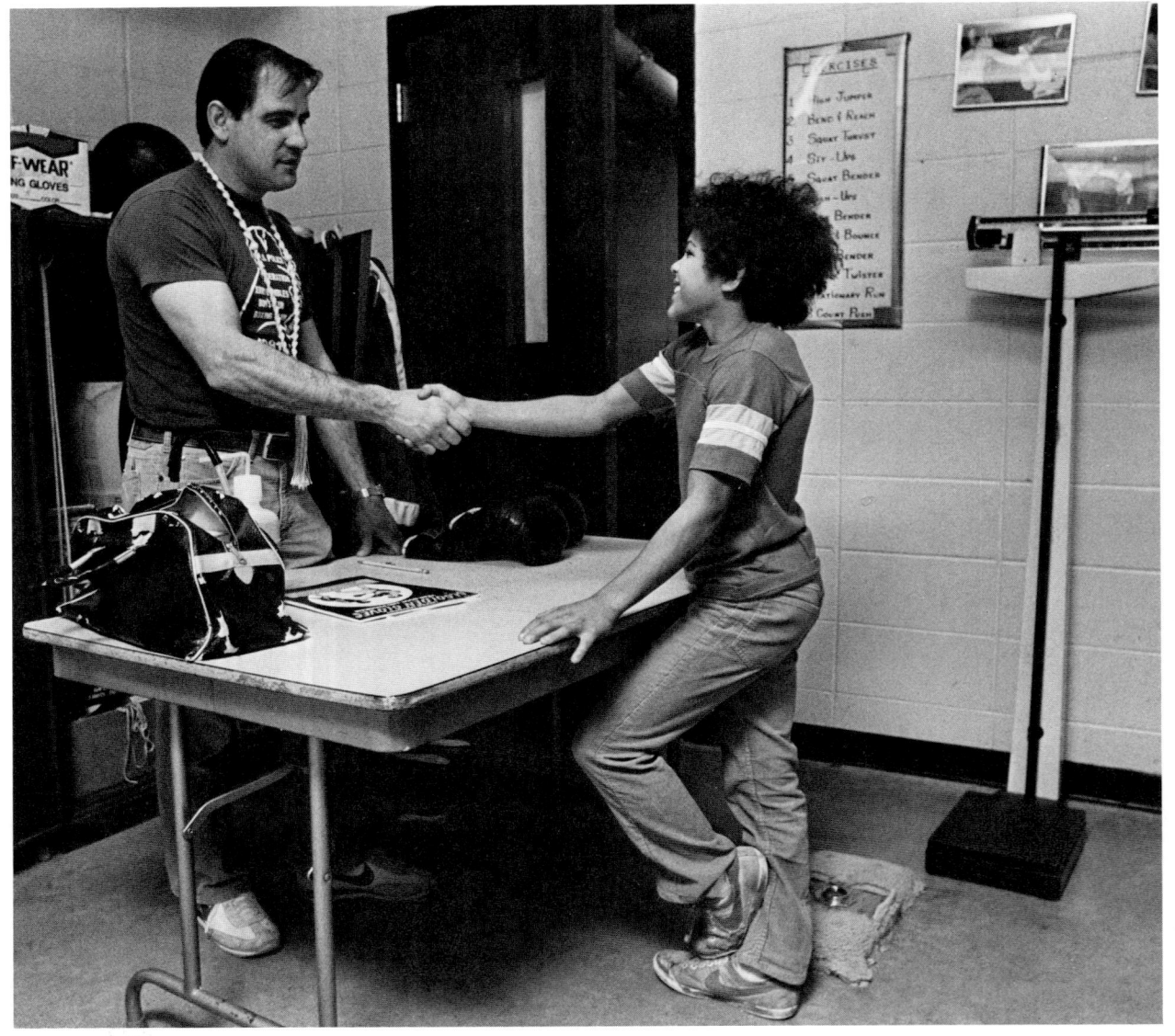

I wanted to know if I could become a boxer, too. So one day I went to the gym and met the boxing coach, Mr. Kelly. He told me that you must be at least 10 years old to learn boxing at the gym. Since I was old enough, Mr. Kelly said I could start right away. He warned me that it would be hard work, but I didn't care. I couldn't wait to get started.

The next day after school I went back to the gym, ready to go to work. I wore tennis shoes, gym shorts, and a T-shirt. Some other boys my age, several older boys, and some men were already there working out. Everyone seemed to know what they were doing. But they were friendly, and I knew they would be helpful.

All the boxers I saw at the gym were in better shape than I was. They said that to become a boxer I would need to develop strength and endurance like they had. So they suggested I start a **conditioning** program to train my body for boxing.

Conditioning includes many exercises, but one of the most important is **roadwork**. Roadwork is running. It builds up speed and endurance. You should spend time jogging for long distances and running **wind sprints**, too. Wind sprints are short distance runs at top speed.

Push-ups and sit-ups are other good conditioning exercises. They build up your stomach and shoulder muscles. We make push-ups harder by doing them with only one arm.

Boxers also train by skipping rope. Rope skipping improves your footwork. And it takes a lot more coordination than I had expected!

Soon I was ready to learn how to **wrap** my hands. Wrapping gives your hands extra support and also prevents injury. Boxers wrap their hands and wrists with long strips of cloth. Most boxers can wrap their own hands. But one of the coaches had to wrap mine for me the first time. These pictures show how wrapping is done.

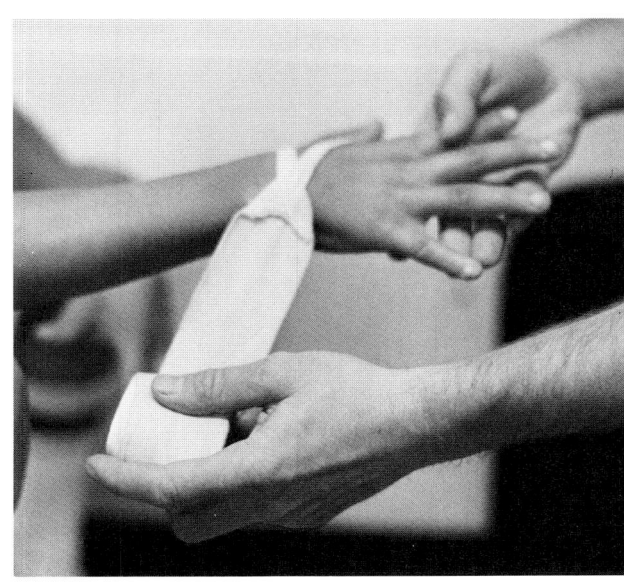 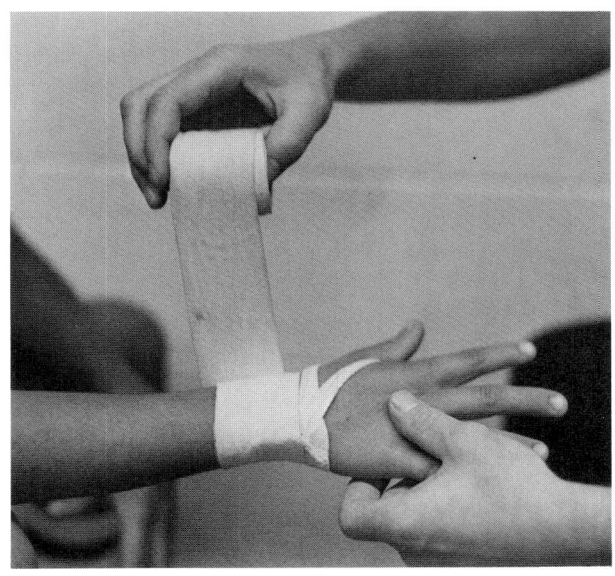

When you are wrapping your hands, hold your fingers apart and your wrist out. One end of the wrap has a small loop. This loop fits over your thumb. From that point, the cloth is wrapped three times around your wrist. Because you start low on the wrist and wind up toward your fingers, each wrap should overlap a little.

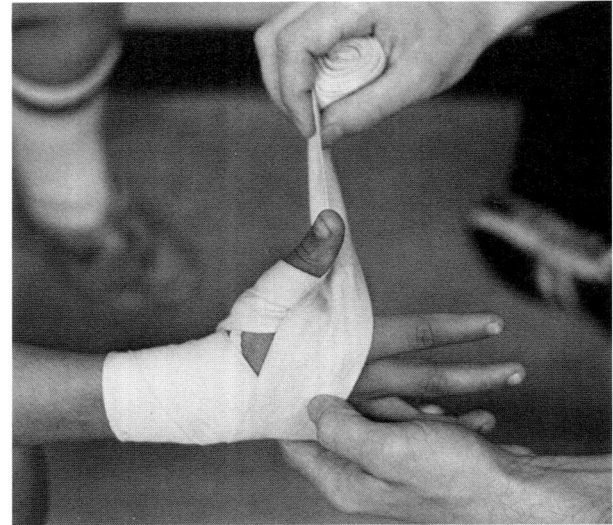
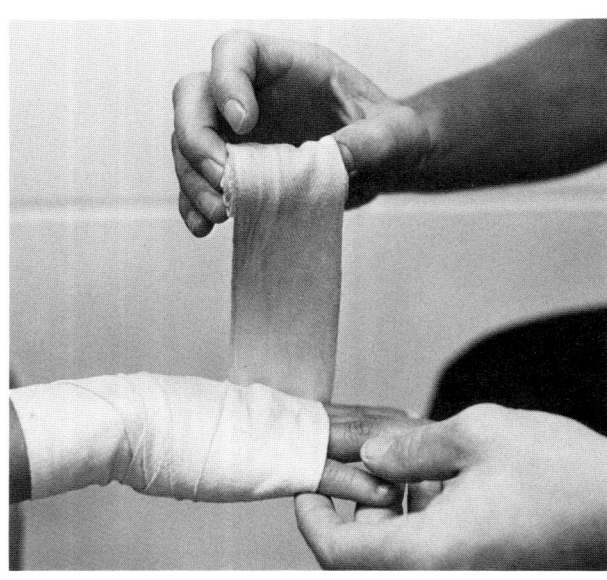
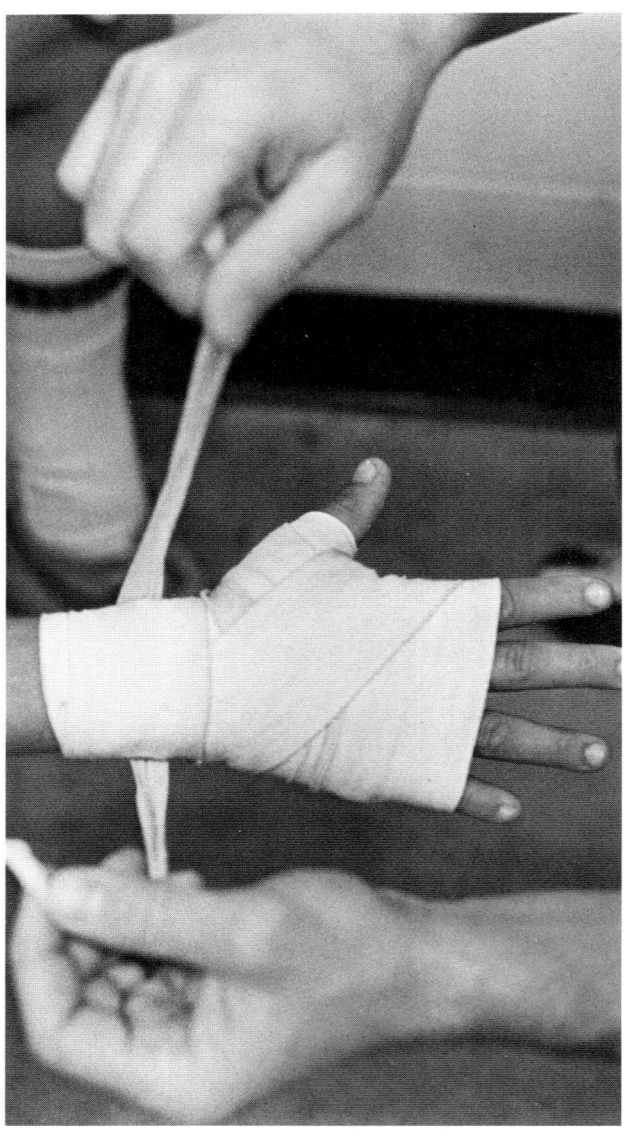

The next wrap brings the cloth around your hand above the thumb. Again, wrap three times. After the third wrap, wind the cloth around your thumb joint. Then three more layers go around your knuckles. Finally, wrap another layer around your thumb joint. You finish by bringing the wrap across the back of your hand, past your little finger, and around your wrist.

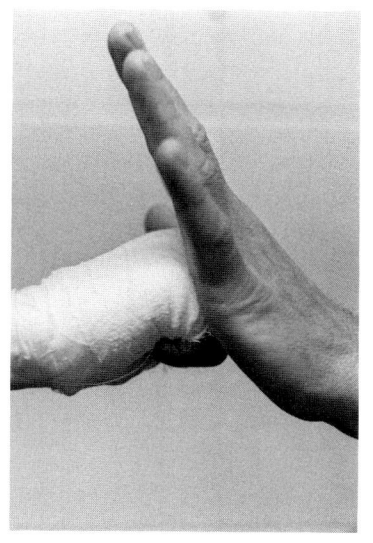

When your hand is wrapped properly, it will feel snug when you make a fist. To make a fist, close all four fingers in your palm. Then put your thumb across all but your little finger. Mr. Kelly said that I should punch only with a tightly closed fist.

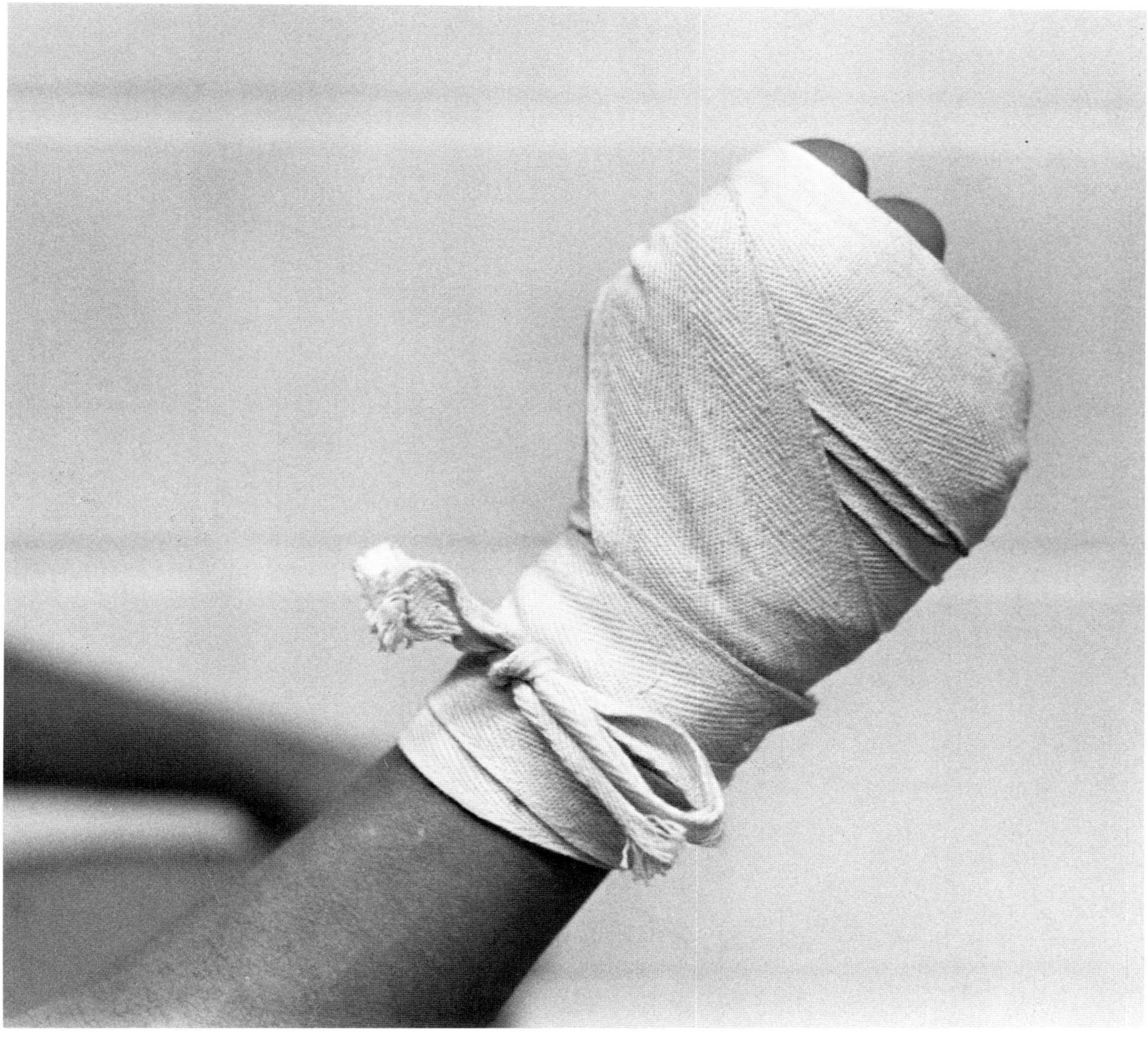

Once my hands were wrapped, I got to put on the boxing gloves. This was the moment I had been looking forward to! The gloves were made of leather. I was surprised at how heavy they felt and how big they looked. The practice gloves weigh 16 ounces. These gloves are soft and less likely to cause injury than the 10-ounce gloves that are used in competition.

I was also given a protective **headgear** to wear. A headgear is like a helmet, and it protects my head and ears from injury. It is important to wear a headgear at all times. The headgear worn during practices is thicker than the headgear worn during an actual bout.

A plastic **mouthpiece** is also worn at all times. The mouthpiece fits over your teeth and protects them from blows. It should be fitted to match the shape of your teeth exactly.

I was really anxious to learn how to punch. But Mr. Kelly said that first I had to learn how to stand and move correctly. He showed me the basic **stance**, or body position. This is the on-guard position you must take between moves.

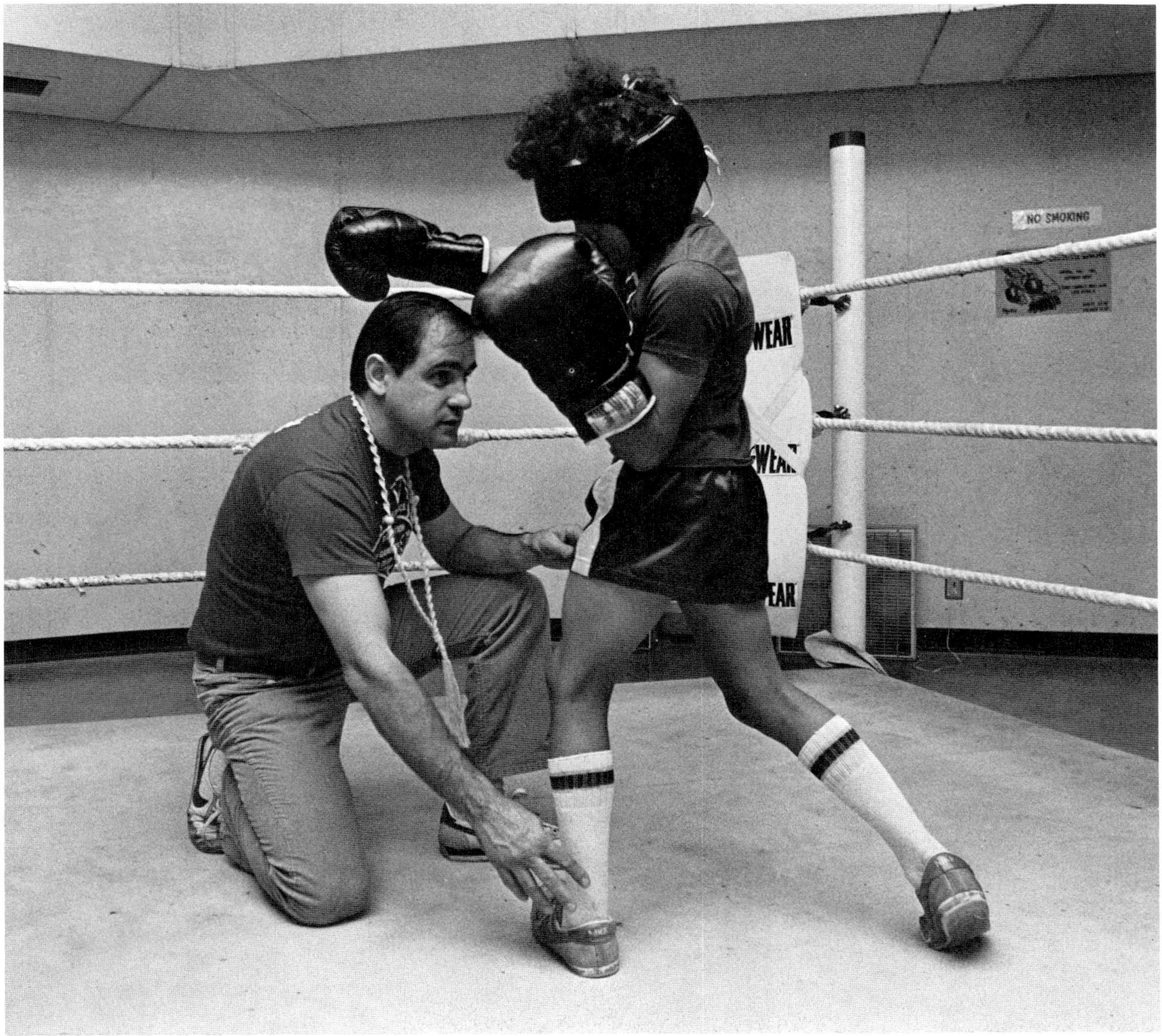

In the basic stance, one foot is ahead of the other. When you shift your weight to the front foot, the heel of your back foot should rise off the floor slightly. The knees should be flexed to keep a springy feeling in the legs.

A good stance will help you move easily in any direction. Move only a few inches, and always move in a sliding motion.

The foot that moves first is called the **lead** (LEED) foot. I learned that the lead foot should be the one that is closest to where I wanted to move. Otherwise I would have to cross my feet, and that could cause me to trip or to lose my balance.

The proper stance also requires good arm positions. Hold your left wrist up at shoulder level and your right fist near your chin. Keep your elbows tucked near your chest to protect your ribs. Your left shoulder should be slightly forward to help protect your chin.

Next I started learning some basic moves. Moving forward is called **advancing**. Moving backwards is called **retreating**. I also practiced **circling**, which is taking small steps to the left or to the right. Mr. Kelly said that I must remember to go back into my basic stance after any move.

After a few more weeks of conditioning and learning moves, I was ready to learn the basics of punching. Mr. Kelly reminded me to keep a good tight fist when I punch. The most important punch for right-handed boxers like me is the **left jab.** A jab is a sharp, quick blow. In the basic stance, your left hand is closer to your opponent, so the left jab can reach your target faster than a punch from the right.

I learned that left-handed boxers, or "southpaws," do their boxing moves by taking steps *opposite* those of a right-handed boxer. For example, the *right* jab is the most important blow for a southpaw.

The left jab extends straight from the shoulder. At the same time that the jab is delivered, you must step forward with your left foot. This stepping action will put the force of your entire body into the punch. Now I understood what Mr. Kelly meant when he said, "The punching has to be done with the entire body. The wrist and fist just carry the power."

LEFT JAB

Turn your fist to the right so that it lands with the knuckle part of the glove. Mr. Kelly said that I should hit "through" my target. This means that I should imagine that my punch will go beyond my target and not stop at my opponent's chin.

If I land the left jab properly, I will be protected from punches from my opponent. My right hand protects the right side of my body, and my left shoulder protects my chin. Although I am protected, I still must move fast and bring my left hand back to the basic position as quickly as possible.

23

At this point I was ready to try practicing moves with a partner. Practicing with a partner is called **sparring**. At first it was hard to remember everything about stance and footwork and to react to my partner's moves at the same time. But he said that the more I practiced, the easier it would become. Soon my moves would be natural, and I would hardly have to think about them.

But my partner warned me that I was developing a bad habit. I had started to **telegraph** the punch. This meant that I drew my hand back a bit before each jab. My partner then knew what was coming, and he could get ready for my punch. I didn't want to get into any bad habits, so I tried hard to stop telegraphing. Now I understood the importance of quick moves!

STRAIGHT RIGHT

The second punch I learned was the **straight right**. This is a powerful punch because of the distance your arm travels. The straight right is done with a full turn of the waist and the shoulders, and it is delivered with a lot of speed. With your whole body behind the punch, it is very effective.

Although your right foot should never leave the floor, the rest of your body turns as the straight right is delivered. When the punch lands, the back of your hand should be facing *up*. Your right shoulder will protect your chin. And your left arm will guard your left side.

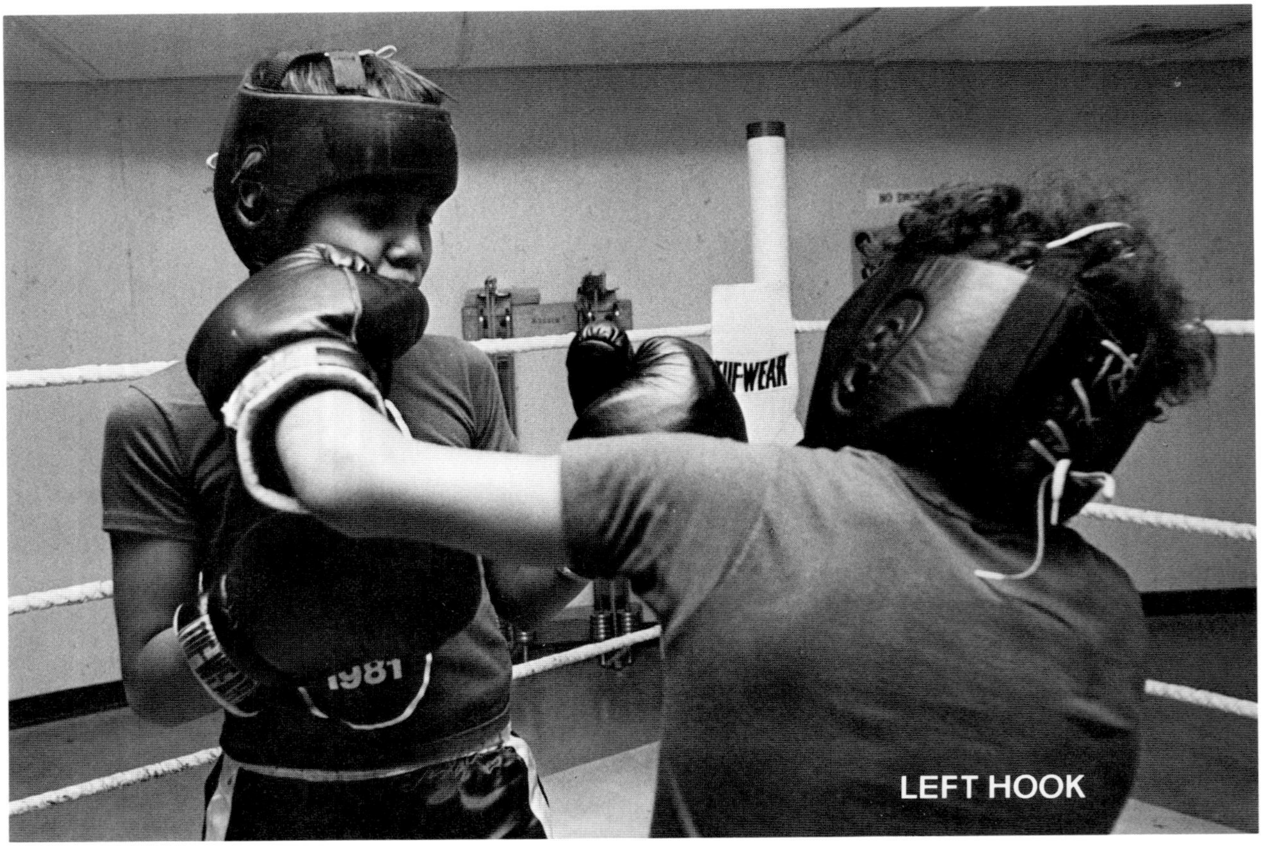

LEFT HOOK

Another basic punch is the **left hook**. A hook is a short, swinging punch that is delivered with a bent arm. In the left hook, your left arm moves in a short curved path toward the target. Your palm faces *in* instead of down, and your left elbow will come away from your body. Unlike the left jab, you do not step forward as you punch. Instead you **pivot**, or turn, toward your opponent on your left foot. Pivoting is the key to the power behind the left hook.

28

The last punch I learned was the **uppercut.** This is a short, swinging punch that is delivered with an upward motion. It is a good punch when you are boxing at close range. Often your target will be your opponent's chin, but it is easier to hit his body.

UPPERCUT

You can deliver an uppercut with either hand, but Mr. Kelly said I should practice with the left hand first. Begin the uppercut by bending at the knees and lowering your left hand. Turn your glove so that the back of your hand faces the floor. When you shoot your fist upward, pivot a bit and straighten your legs. This leg action is what gives the punch its power.

I learned that two or three of the same punches thrown quickly one after the other can be very effective. So I learned how to put different moves together in **combinations.** The punches are given numbers. A left jab is number one, a straight right is number two, and a left hook is number three.

LEFT JAB

STRAIGHT RIGHT

The most common combination is a one-two, which is a left jab followed by a straight right.

I practiced punches and combinations with Shane, another boy at the gym. Shane is a good sparring partner because he is about my size and weight.

Every time your boxing partner throws a punch, he creates an opening with his arms where you can punch back. Punching back during an attack is called **countering**.

COUNTERING

You want to be fast enough so that your counter punch reaches your opponent before his blow reaches you. But this takes a lot of concentration and good timing.

There are other ways of avoiding your opponent's punches, too. I was anxious to learn these **defensive** moves.

DUCKING

Ducking is one way to defend yourself against a punch. To duck punches from your opponent's left hand, simply bend at the knees and waist. Then step in toward your opponent and keep your hands up to guard your body. To duck punches from your opponent's right hand, simply lean back or to the side. But be careful not to lose your balance.

BLOCKING

Blocking is another defensive skill. Blocking is using your arms and gloves to take blows. This protects your body and head from being hit. You can block with your left arm and elbow, for example, to keep your opponent's right punch from reaching your body.

PARRYING

I also learned how to **parry** a punch. To parry means to deflect, or push away, a blow. You use your glove and arm to force your opponent's arm to the outside. I discovered that parrying does not require much strength. But it does take good timing to catch the punch before it reaches you.

You don't always need a partner to practice boxing. You can practice punches on a **heavy bag.** A heavy bag is a large canvas or leather bag stuffed with a man-made material. You can punch it with a lot of force. When working on the heavy bag, you wear special gloves called **bag gloves.** They give extra protection to the knuckles and soften the blows.

I really loved boxing, and I practiced hard almost every day. As I became a better boxer, I decided to enter the city's Golden Gloves competition. This is a competition for amateur boxers. Boxers at my age level are in the junior division. Our matches are sometimes called the Junior Olympics.

Matches in the junior division are made up of three 1½-minute **rounds**. We get a 1-minute rest between rounds. Once the round has started, there are no time outs. If a boxer is tired, he will **clinch** to gain time.

CLINCH

Clinching is holding your opponent's arms under yours so that he cannot use them. You must hold tight. But try not to wrestle, because that will make you even more tired. A referee will stop a clinch by calling, "Break." When this happens, the boxers must move apart. Carefully take one full step backward.

A boxing match is held in a roped-off, square platform called a **ring**. The floor of the ring is padded and is covered with canvas. Because there are a number of important rules to remember during a bout, boxers are watched carefully by the referee. The referee is the only other person inside the ring besides the boxers.

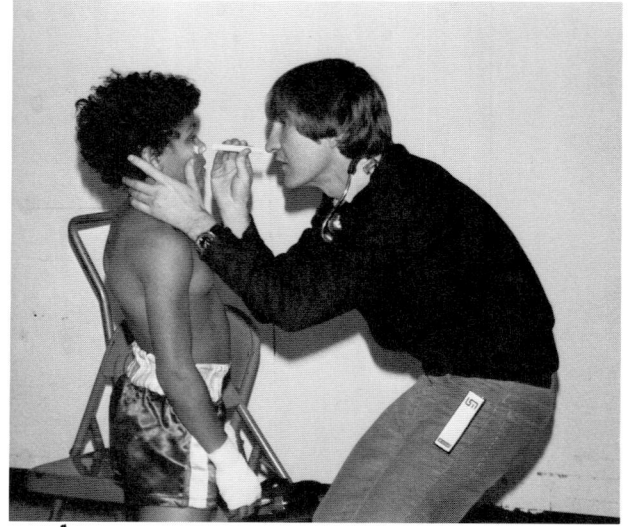
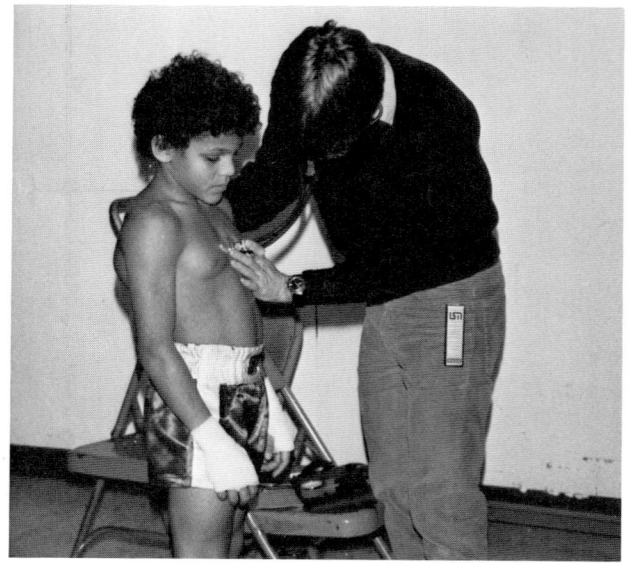

As the Golden Gloves got closer, I trained harder than ever. Everyone at the gym helped me. They were just as excited as I was, because they would be boxing in the competition, too. Before the match, I went to the gym's doctor for a complete physical. He told me I was healthy. The doctor would be at ringside during the bout just in case anyone was hurt.

Before my match, Mr. Kelly went over the most important rules with me. He reminded me not to commit any **fouls**, such as hitting my opponent below the belt, hitting with the back of my hand, or wrestling. Good sportsmanship is important in boxing. Opponents always shake hands after a bout.

I was nervous on the night of my match. My parents and the other boxers from the gym would be watching. I tried to think about the match and not the audience.

My match was against a boy named Andrew. He had been boxing much longer than I had. But Mr. Kelly said not to worry. He said that if I stuck with the basics, I would do fine.

I tried to remember to vary my punches and to deliver combinations. I landed several left jabs. Andrew landed some punches, too, when I dropped my right hand. So I quickly went into a clinch to gain a few seconds and to recover from the blows.

I was trying to land most of my punches in the **scoring area**. This is the area from my opponent's hairline down to his waist. Scoring is done on a **20-point-must** system. The winner automatically gets 20 points. The loser can have 19 points or below. In boxing, three blows to the scoring area equal 1 point. There are five judges who do the scoring.

Our rounds were only 1½ minutes long. But they sure seemed longer than that when I was in the ring! I was more tired after the first round than I had been after any of my workouts.

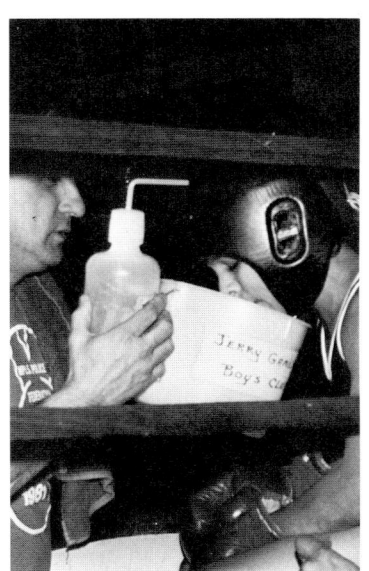
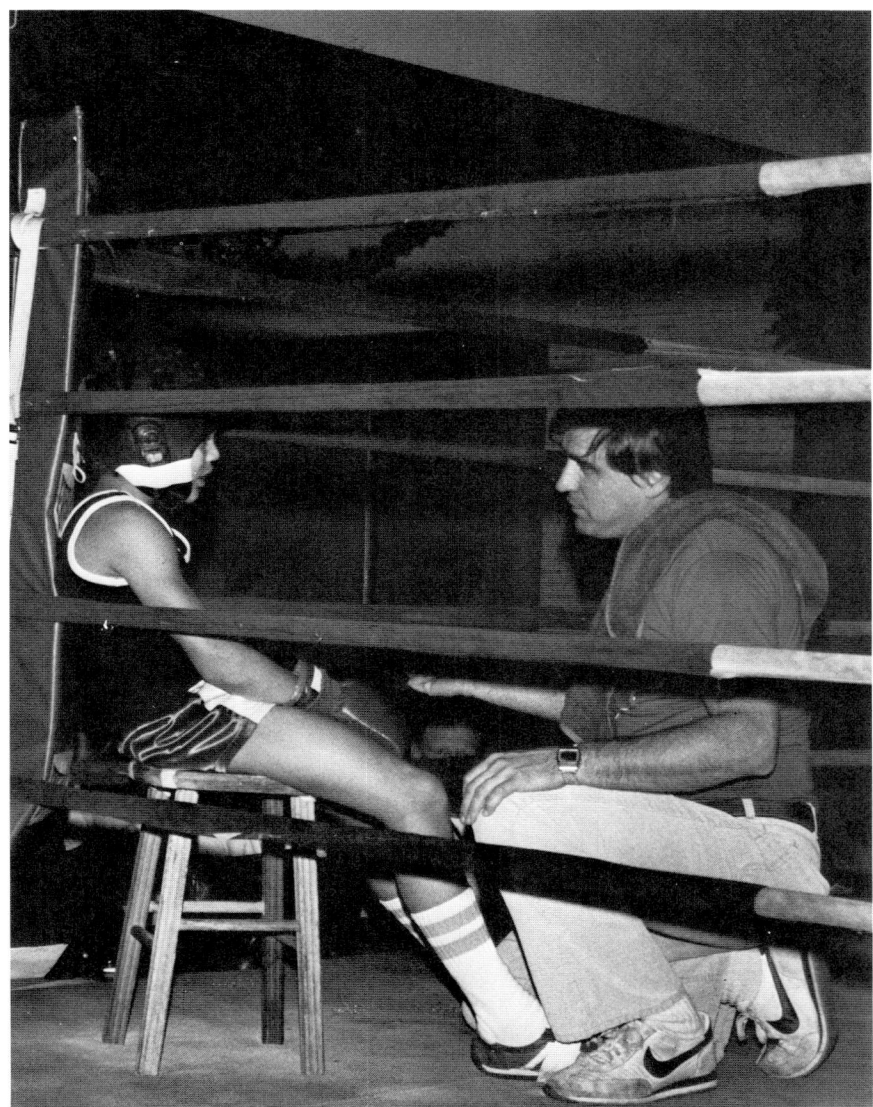

During my 1-minute rest period, Mr. Kelly gave me some water and told me that I was doing fine. He told me to keep bobbing and weaving, because my opponent would have a harder time hitting a moving target.

Soon the match was over. The judges added their scorecards, and I found out that I was the loser. I was pretty disappointed, but I shook hands with the winner. I was glad that I had gotten in a lot of punches. I knew that I had done my best.

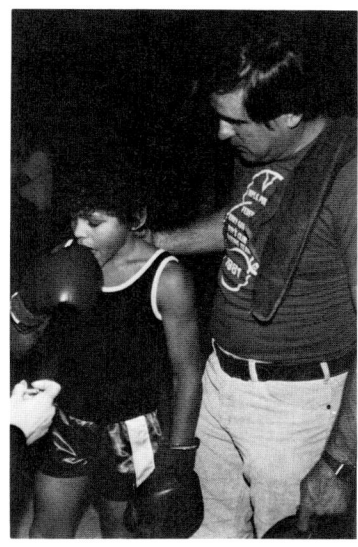

After the match, Mr. Kelly and I talked about how I had done. He told me some of the things that I had done well. And he pointed out some of my mistakes. He said that with more conditioning and more experience, I would do even better next year. I hope so, because boxing *is* for me!

Words about BOXING

ADVANCE: To move toward your opponent

AMATEUR: An athlete who does not earn money for competing in sports

BELL: The gong used to signal the start and end of a round

BLOCK: To use your arms and gloves to prevent a punch from landing

BREAK: The referee's order to end a clinch. The boxers must step apart.

CIRCLE: To take small steps to the left or to the right

CLINCH: To hold your opponent's arms under yours so that he cannot punch

COUNTER: To prevent a blow by landing a punch of your own

DEFENSIVE MOVE: A move used to guard yourself from your opponent

DUCK: To draw back or to lean away from the punch to prevent a punch from landing

FEINT: A faked punch used to catch your opponent off guard

KNOCKOUT (KO) When a boxer is knocked down and is unable to get up within 10 seconds

LEAD (LEED) FOOT: The foot that moves first

LEFT HOOK: A short, curved punch delivered with the left hand

LEFT JAB: A straight punch delivered with the left hand

OFFENSIVE MOVE: An attacking move

PARRY: To use your glove and arm to push away an opponent's punch

REFEREE STOPS CONTEST (RSC): When a fight is stopped by a referee because of an injury or to prevent a more serious injury to one of the boxers

RETREAT: To move away from your opponent

RING: A square, roped-off platform in which matches take place

ROUND: The time periods in a match. In the junior division, a match consists of three rounds, each 1½ minutes long.

SHADOW BOXING: To practice with an imaginary opponent

SOUTHPAW: Slang term for a left-handed boxer

SPAR: To practice boxing in a ring with another boxer

STANCE: The position of the body and feet when a boxer is on guard

UPPERCUT: A curved punch in which the fist travels upward

J 796 .83 T   4-6
Thomas, Art, 1952-
Boxing is for me

DATE DUE		
	DISCARDED FROM THE	
	PORTVILLE FREE LIBRARY	

PORTVILLE FREE LIBRARY

PORTVILLE, N. Y.

Member Of
Chautauqua-Cattaraugus Library System